DIARY
OF A
MINECRAFT
ZOMBIE

Book 6

Zack Zombie

Sunday

One more week and I'm off to camp.

I kinda have mixed feelings about it.

I really don't want to go, because I would rather stay home and play video games and eat cake every day for the whole summer.

But, my friend Creepy feels really lonely at camp, not to mention that he gets picked on by the other kids.

That burns me up and makes me feel like I have to be there for him.

So, I'm going to camp in the Swamp Biome for the next three weeks, not knowing if I'm going to come back alive.

You see, I think the camp counselors are really brain eating humans that are just waiting for the next batch of mob kids to fill their bottomless stomachs.

Also, I've heard rumors of the cafeteria food coming to life and terrorizing campers.

I thought the camp nurse was a rotten flesh eating witch, too. But I met her recently and she seems pretty normal.

…Or, maybe she's only normal when she's at her normal job? What if she changes at camp and becomes a hideous she-demon that eats zombie kids for breakfast?

Wow. I don't think I want to go to camp anymore.

Sorry, Creepy, you're on your own.

What am I thinking?

I need to be a good friend. And good friends are there when you need them.

So, I guess I'm going to camp.

At least the good thing I can look forward to is that Steve is coming too.

So, I guess if I die, I won't be alone.

Monday

Today my Mom and Dad took me to get some camping gear for my trip to camp.

I thought we were getting a couple of diamond swords, some armor, a bow and arrow, a Redstone machine gun, a pickaxe, and a shovel in case I need to bury some of the counselors and hide their bodies.

...You can't be too careful when you're going to war.

But Mom and Dad just laughed at me when I told them about all of the dangers I was going to face at camp.

Why is it that parents never take kids seriously?

One day, some kid somewhere is going to declare the next Human Apocalypse, and parents are going to say, "Ha ha, you're so funny, junior!" And then get eaten by some brain eating humans.

And I'm going to be there to say, "See, that's what you get!"

Just sayin'.

But me, I'm going to be prepared.

If my parents aren't going to get me the weapons I need, I'm going to have to get them somewhere else.

And I know who to get them from too.

I can always count on Steve for stuff like that, and I'm sure he has an arsenal in his basement or something.

Mom can waste her time on maggot spray and Zombie-wipes.

…but I am really glad she never forgets to pack the cookies and milk.

Tuesday

Another good thing about going to camp is that I don't have to be around my little brother for three weeks.

Don't get me wrong. I love my little brother. I just don't *like* him very much.

I mean he's cute and fun sometimes, but most of the time he's so annoying.

He always takes my stuff, and then he breaks it.

When we play video games, Mom always makes me play the games he likes.

And he also gets away with everything. Like when we get into a fight, Mom and Dad always take his side.

They say that I should be nicer to him because he's only four years old, but I know the truth. I know that he's possessed by the spirit of a sixteen year old human demon, and only I can see it.

But the part I hate the most about my little brother is that before he was born my Mom and Dad gave me all of their attention.

Now, they give him all of the attention.

Sometimes I don't mind, because I don't want my parent's attention all of the time.

But when I do want their attention, they're either busy working or playing with my little brother.

It's kinda lonely sometimes.

So, I guess three weeks away from my little brother is worth going to camp.

Even if I am entering into a war of epic proportions.

Hmmm. Maybe I should take my little brother with me and use him as a zombie shield?

Naah, he's too small. I'll probably still get eaten.

I could use him as ammo for my zombie catapult though…

Wednesday

I went to go visit Steve today to talk about our strategy for surviving camp.

I went to our usual spot, but I couldn't find him.

I walked by some bushes, when all of a sudden…

"HHEEEAAHHHHHHH!!!!"

"AAAHHHH!!!" I yelled.

Steve jumped out of the bushes, all dressed in green and brown paint.

"Hey Zombie!" Steve said.

"What'd you do that for?!!" I said. "You scared the life out of me!"

"But I thought you were dead?" Steve said.

"Forget it. What's up with the outfit?" I asked.

"I put it together so that we can hide out and catch our enemies by surprise," Steve said. "I've got some more green and brown paint for you too."

"Don't worry about me," I said, "After that scare, I think I made enough green and brown paint to last me the whole summer."

"So Steve, what kind of weapons do you have? I think we're going to need as many as we can get against those brain eating camp counselors and the cafeteria food monster."

"Honestly, I don't have any," he said. "I just have my pickaxe, but I used it so much that the durability is almost gone."

"Aw, Man. What are we going to do? We're going to be defenseless," I said.

"Not totally," Steve said. "I still have my crafting table. I bet if we brought it with us, we can craft some cool tools and weapons at the Swamp Biome."

"Also, we could make some TNT," Steve added.

"Whoa. How do you make it?"

"Well, you need sand and gunpowder," he said. "I have plenty of sand but I need gunpowder."

"Where do you get it?" I asked him.

"Well, you can get it from a dungeon chest. But that'll take forever to find," he said.

"Is there anywhere else you can get it?" I asked.

"You can also get it from killing a Ghast or a Creeper," he said.

We both looked at each other for a minute.

"Naah," we both said.

So we're going into battle with only a crafting table, a weak pickaxe, and plenty of green and brown paint.

Not much of a defense, but it's going to have to do.

Creepaway Camp, here we come!

OORAH!

Thursday

Today, after dinner, my parents had a talk with me about what to expect when I go to camp.

I didn't really need the talk, because Steve and I were already mounting a strong defense against the evils that were waiting for us on the Creepaway Camp battle front.

But I decided to play along anyway.

"Zombie, you're going to be away from home for an entire three weeks. That's the longest you've ever been away from us," my Mom said.

"Uh huh."

"We think it's good for you because it will help you become more self-reliant, and you will learn how to work together with other kids and adults."

The only adults I'm going to work with are the camp counselors Steve and I will be interrogating.

"You'll also have to learn how to "rough it" son," Dad said. "Kind of like when you and I go on our camping trips. That means no video games, no television, and no computer for three whole weeks."

What?

"But you'll have plenty of time to read, and plenty of time to write letters to your friends," Mom said. "And you'll also have plenty of time to make crafts, which I'm sure you'll like."

Wait a minute. No video games. No television. No computer. Reading and writing every day. And making crafts? I'm not sure I'm ready for this.

"Now, you may feel a little homesick," Dad said.

"What's that?... That's good, right?" I asked.

"Well, feeling homesick means that you'll really want to come home," he said.

Man, I feel that way right now, and I haven't even gone to camp yet.

"But don't worry, I'm sure you'll have so much fun, that you'll forget all about it," Dad added, as he shared a look with my mom.

Wow, that was supposed to be a pep talk, but I feel worse than ever.

How am I supposed to get through three weeks without video games, television or my computer?

This feels more like prison camp.

Man, this is going to be a lot harder than I thought.

Friday

Well, today is my last day of freedom.

Tomorrow, I face the horrors of war, as I come face to face with my enemies at Creepaway Camp.

I may not make it back alive.

But I go knowing that my friend Creepy is counting on me, and I won't let him down.

Not to mention, I carry on my shoulders the fate of every mob kid that will ever go to Creepaway Camp.

If I fail, the camp counselors will feast on the brains of countless mob kids for years to come.

And the cafeteria monster will have its fill of the remains.

But if I win, with the help of my trusted friend Steve, we will change the face of history, and make camp the best place to be all summer.

Our battle may go down in history as the greatest battle ever fought.

We may even create a national holiday for it too.

And from our victory, we will give the power back to the kids, and make camp a place for kids, run by kids.

Then we'll call it what it should've been called in the first place: "Play Video Games and Eat Cake All Day Camp."

Bring it!

Saturday

I got up really early today and brought my stuff downstairs.

My Mom, Dad, and little bro were waiting for me by the door.

"Goodbye, son," my mom said, as her eye sockets welled up with tears.

"This will be good for him, honey," my Dad said. "A few weeks in the Swamp Biome will really put some mold on his chest."

Since this was the last time I was going to see my parents before going off to war, I thought it was OK to give them a hug.

I was going to say goodbye to my little brother, but he was busy running around on his chicken.

"Wesley, come say goodbye to your big brother," my Mom said.

"Bye Bye, Zombie," my little brother said. "I hope you don't die."

I still thought my little brother would make great ammo for my zombie catapult, but I knew my Mom wouldn't go for it.

"Goodbye, little bro," I said.

You know I actually think I'm going to miss the little minion.

When I got outside, the bus had just arrived.

All I could see was a bunch of mob kids looking through the window, each with a look on their face that said, "*Yeah, we're doomed.*"

I tried to look brave, but I was just as scared as the other kids.

When I got on the bus, I saw Creepy at the back.

"Zombie! Sit back here next to me!" he said.

I started making my way to the back when all of a sudden a skeleton foot came out of nowhere and tripped me.

I hit the floor of the bus with my face.

It's a good thing I don't have a nose, I thought.

Then all of the camp kids started laughing.

When I got up, there was a Wither Skeleton boy pointing at me and laughing.

Man, another bully, I thought.

When I got to the back of the bus, Creepy looked at me like he knew what I was going through.

"I see you met Nick," Creepy said. "He's one of the kids that bullies me every year at camp."

Great, a Wither Skeleton named Nick is going to bother me for the next three weeks at camp. What else could go wrong?

Then Creepy started hissing again…

Saturday Evening

It's a good thing that Creepy brought his liquid Nitrogen inhaler with him. Otherwise all the mob kids would be traveling to camp in body bags.

Don't get me wrong, body bags are fun. I just don't think they packed enough for all of us.

When we finally got to the camp in the Swamp Biome, it was already late.

We were welcomed by all the camp counselors. I figured they were trying to size us up to see which one of us had the biggest brains to eat first.

I wore a Zombie baseball cap so they wouldn't think that just because I had a big

26

square head, I carried the biggest Zombie brains.

"Welcome Campers," the head Zombie Counselor said. "My name is Jerry, Jerry Carcass, and I am the head counselor at Camp Cobblestone, the best Creepaway Camp this side of the Swamp Biome. I would like to let you know that we are very happy that all of you have joined us, and we are looking forward to feeding those young brains of yours this summer."

You mean feeding 'on' our young brains, I thought.

"You have all been assigned a head counselor who will help familiarize you with camp life…"

"Did he say *tenderize* you?" I asked Creepy.

"What?" Creepy said.

"And, we are looking forward to all of you helping us beat the pants off of our rival camp down the road, Camp Nether Rack, at our Camp Moblympics games in a few weeks," he said.

"BOOOOOOO!!" yelled Nick, the Wither Skeleton.

"What's eating him?" I asked Creepy.

"Nick used to go to Camp Nether Rack, but he got kicked out for poisoning somebody," Creepy said. "Now I think he takes it out on all of the kids here."

"Thank you, campers! And we're look forward to having you over for breakfast tomorrow evening, bright and early," Jerry said.

"Did he say *having you for breakfast*?" I asked Creepy.

28

"Zombie, why are you so jumpy?" Creepy asked.

"I just want to be ready when the first wave attacks, that's all," I said.

Creepy just looked at me…confused.

Sunday

BANG! BANG! BANG!

"Rise and shine campers!"

"Uuurrggh-huh?!!!"

"Time to get up and take in that fresh stale Swamp air!" the camp counselor said.

"What time is it?" one of the campers said.

"It's sundown!" I said. "Man, I never get up before night time."

I could tell that none of the mob kids in my cabin ever got up that early either.

The mob kids in my cabin are real cool. Me and Creepy are together with two other guys.

There's Endy, who's an Enderman.

Last night we were all asking him to teleport. But he hasn't learned how to do it yet. He said that all of the other kids his age can teleport, but for some reason he can't.

Endy also has some pet Endermites that he brought with him to camp. I think they're kind of weird looking, but Endy likes them.

And then there's Flapper. He's a Guardian from the Ocean Biome, which is kinda weird because we all thought Guardians couldn't live outside of water.

But Flapper said that was just a myth. He said that Guardians can breathe in air and underwater. He said he's *am-fi-bee-us*, whatever that means.

Flapper is kinda funny looking, though. He doesn't have arms and legs so he just flaps around to get from place to place.

He also has one big eye that looks like it's following you around all the time.

Creepy said that our cabins usually have five mob kids, but for some reason ours only had four, until...

"You guys have one more addition to your cabin," the counselor said.

All of a sudden, Nick, the Wither Skeleton walked in.

All of us looked at each other with a look that said, *Yup, we're dead*.

"You guys get acquainted, and I will see you all at roll call," the camp counselor said.

"What's up, Cretans?" Nick said. "Let me see, I think I'm going to take this bunk," he said as he threw Endy's stuff on the floor.

I helped Endy pick up his stuff and find another bunk.

Creepy was trying to be friendly, so he asked Nick, "Hey Nick, how come you're coming to our cabin this year? You never choose Cabin Zero."

"Why do you care, Cretan?" he said. "But if you want to know, I got kicked out of my other cabin, because one of the kids blamed me for poisoning his pet squid."

"Did you do it?" Creepy asked.

"Well, if you keep asking questions, you're gonna find out," Nick said.

This is going to a long three weeks, I thought.

After roll call, the camp counselors had a cabin inspection.

The messiest cabin got to be first in line for breakfast.

Well, I didn't want to be the first to be cafeteria monster chow, so I had to make sure our cabin would lose the inspection.

So while the counselors were checking the other cabins, I ran to my cabin.

What could I do to make sure we fail this inspection?

I know!

34

After all five of us went in the bathroom earlier, we were sure to win the cabin inspection with the mess we left in there.

So I flushed the toilet to make sure we would lose. They probably wouldn't expect to see a clean toilet in a mob kid's cabin.

Worked like a charm!

We were the last ones to get in the breakfast line.

The cafeteria food monster must have been full after eating the other mob kids. Because when we got to the cafeteria, I didn't see any mob kid body parts or remains.

Man, that monster must've picked those kids clean, I thought.

I found the other kids in my cabin and sat with them to eat.

I made sure not to eat the food in case it had monster eggs. I can imagine them hatching in my stomach and then some monster bursting out of my chest.

"I'm really sad that we failed our cabin inspection," Creepy said.

"Yeah," Endy said. "I spent like an hour and four comic books trying to make sure the bathroom would help us win for sure."

Those young campers, I thought, *they are so inexperienced with the horrors of war.* I didn't have the heart to tell them the truth.

"Don't worry guys," I said. "It will all work out in the end."

They don't know how close they came to certain death at the hands of the cafeteria food monster, I thought.

Then Flapper the Guardian flapped over to our table.

"Hey guys, did you hear about the talent show they're having at the end of camp?" he said. "We should totally do something."

"I can play drums, " Creepy said.

We all looked at each other confused, especially since Creepy doesn't have any arms.

"I can play the Note Blocks," Endy said. "My mom made me take lessons."

"I can jump on a tambourine," Flapper said. "But we still need somebody to play guitar and sing. How about you, Zombie?"

"I can do a mean air guitar," I said, "so playing a real guitar can't be that hard."

"That settles it, let's make a band!" Flapper said.

All of us were really happy to be in the talent show. But we still needed a singer.

Hmmm, I wonder if Steve can sing.

Monday

Man, it's only been two days and I already miss my video games, my computer and my TV.

I still don't know why parents would be OK sending their kids away to be tortured like this.

The camp counselors tried to take our minds off of the screen by filling the day with activities.

But I could tell it wasn't working.

I saw a Zombie kid with a dazed look on his face as he walked around, moving his hands like he was using his video game controller.

Another kid made a video game console out of his macaroni art, and he kept trying to play it.

And at lunch, another mob kid turned his food into a video game!

This kind of torture is just pure evil...

Tuesday

Today we ran the craziest obstacle course ever.

We had to climb walls, crawl under wire, climb up ropes, do parkour, and walk through mud.

But the scariest part was when they made us climb some swamp vines. And they made us do it over water!

Some of the mob kids got so scared that they fell apart.

The camp counselors had to take them to the infirmary to see if they could put them back together.

When it was my turn to do it, I got halfway across, and then I got so scared I froze.

All the kids were laughing at me. And the other camp counselors were yelling at me to hurry up.

But I was too scared to move.

All of a sudden, one of the camp counselors climbed on the vine next to me and started talking to me.

"What's your name?" he said.

"My name is Zack...but my friends call me Zombie," I said.

"Hey Zombie," he said. "My name is Billy, Billy Carrion."

"Uh huh."

"Zombie, you know what? I used to be a camper here a few years ago too," he said.

"Really?"

"Yeah, and you know, when I had to do the Vine Cross, I was so nervous that I lost my head," he said.

"For real?"

"Yeah, came clean off. And my body was still stuck up here on the vine. It took them two days to get my body down," he said. "After that, all the kids called me Headless all summer."

Just thinking about Billy's body stuck up on the vine without a head made me laugh.

"Feel better?" he asked.

"Yeah, I guess I do."

"How about we climb the rest of the way, and we grab a few booger snacks after," he said.

"Uh, Ok."

So I climbed the rest of the way till I made it to the end.

Afterwards, Creepy, Endy and Flapper ran up to me.

"Are you alright, Zombie?" they all asked.

"Yeah, I'm OK," I said.

"Man, the first time I went on the Vine Cross I got stuck up there too," Creepy said. "Billy helped me get down too. Billy said that if I ever feel afraid, that I should just think of something funny to make the fear go away. When I do the Vine Cross now, I just imagine Billy's headless Zombie body up on the vine for two days, and it helps me get through it real fast."

I was going to ask Creepy how he does the Vine Cross without any arms. But what I really wanted to know was why Billy could be so nice, especially since he was one of the

44

bloodthirsty camp counselors that were out to eat our brains.

Confusing...

Wednesday

Today I had to go to the Nurse's office because I hurt myself while doing some team building exercises.

We did a team building exercise called the Trust exercise.

I had to close my eye sockets and fall backward, and my cabin mates were supposed to catch me.

I don't think the camp counselors thought that one through very well.

Since Creepy and Flapper didn't have any arms, the only ones left to catch me were Endy and Nick, the Wither Skeleton.

Endy and Nick were supposed to hold hands, but right when I fell, Nicked pulled away and I fell smack on the floor.

Man, it hurt.

The nurse was the same nurse I saw the last day of school at the carnival.

She was really nice too, which was confusing, since she was supposed to be a rotten flesh eating witch that could swallow you whole.

"Hey Zombie," she said, "it's good to see you again."

"Hi, Nurse Golem," I said.

I was looking around to see if I could find any of her instruments of torture, but I couldn't see any.

She must have them in a hidden chamber behind a secret wall, I thought.

47

"Looks like you got a nasty bump on your head," she said, "Good for you. A few more of those and you'll be the best looking Zombie at camp."

"Thanks, Nurse Golem," I said.

I wanted to ask her if she was a rotten flesh eating witch, but I thought she might eat me whole because I had discovered her evil plan.

"Nurse Golem…" I said.

"Yes, Zombie?

"Nuthin…" I said.

I went back to my cabin, trying to figure out why the camp counselors and the nurse were being so nice to me.

Oh no! I thought. *They must want to put a spell on me so that afterward, I can lead the other unsuspecting kids toward their doom!*

Diabolical, I thought.

48

Well, it's not going to work.

I'm sure there's some sort of potion to ward off a witch's curse.

I'll ask Steve. He gets here on Saturday. I'm sure he'll know what to do...

Thursday

Today they took the kids cave exploring so we can discover our *true selves*, whatever that means.

I've been in caves like a million times. So I thought this cave trip would be as boring as ever.

Except these caves were different. The camp counselor told us that we were going to a cave that had a recently discovered Stronghold in it.

Strongholds are really cool, because it's like the only place you can find an End Portal.

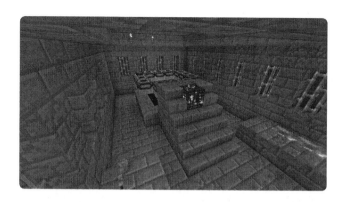

Endy was really excited about the trip. He said the End Portal was how his family first emigrated to our world. He said his grandparents told him all kinds of stories about it when he was a little kid.

I thought it was cool too, because there is only one other End Portal that has ever been found.

The person guiding us on the tour was a famous archaeologist mob Skeleton lady, named Lara Craft.

Before we went in, she made us wear helmets so that we wouldn't get hit by falling cave stones and stuff.

So, after exploring the caves for a few hours, we finally arrived at the Stronghold. It was awesome.

There were all kind of cool rooms in there. There was a room with a fountain, a room with a pillar in it, and a library.

We found all kind of chests inside with cool stuff, too. But they didn't let us keep the stuff we found.

I was bummed too because Endy had found some Redstone in one chest, Flapper found a Gold ingot, and Creepy found a pickaxe that he had trouble picking up.

In the library, I found a chest with an Enchanted Book.

This might come in handy against the camp counselors, the witch nurse and the cafeteria monster, I thought.

So I decided to hide it and keep it to myself.

But Nick saw me hide it, which I knew meant trouble.

"What you got there, Cretan?" Nick asked me.

"Nothing," I said.

"Looks like a book," he said. "What are you going to give me so I don't tell the camp counselors that you took it?"

Oh man, here comes the blackmail. Why is it that bullies always have to blackmail you? They're probably practicing so when they grow up they'll make good mobsters.

"What do you want?" I asked him.

"Well, if anybody gets poisoned in our cabin, I want you to take the blame for it," he said.

"You planning on poisoning somebody?" I asked.

"Well, it's not like I can help it," he said. "It just keeps happening in my sleep. And my parents warned me that if I poisoned anyone else that I would get in real trouble."

"Why don't you go to a witch doctor for that?" I asked him. "We are in the Swamp Biome, you know."

"Look Cretan, it's none of your business. And if you tell anyone, then everybody is going to know about your special book, got it?!!" he said.

"Yeah, I got it," I said.

So for the rest of the trip, Nick just gave me a look to tell me he owned me.

But I didn't care, because with the Enchanted Book, I could ward off any spells the nurse witch or camp counselors could use on me.

Friday

Today was official prank day.

This is the day that the camp counselors allow the mob kids to prank each other as much as they want.

But what usually happens is that all the cabins with the tough kids usually prank all the cabins with the nice kids.

The good thing about having Nick, the Wither Skeleton in our cabin, is that nobody would dare prank our cabin.

The only problem? I It was open season for Nick to prank all of us.

First thing, we all woke up to Flapper screaming and yelling.

Since Flapper was in the bottom bunk, Nick had created two walls out of duct tape and locked Flapper in.

We could hear Flapper screaming and yelling and flapping in his bunk.

It took us a while, but we got him out.

But we were all scared because we knew we were next.

Later, me and the guys were in our cabin reading comics during the morning break.

All of a sudden we saw the door open and somebody chucked like 12 cans of shaving cream in the cabin, all tied to a small block of TNT.

After the explosion, all of us were white from head to toe.

After we got cleaned up, we tried to get out of the cabin to go to lunch. I didn't even get through the door because Nick had covered the top part of the door with plastic wrap. Almost took my head off.

After lunch, Endy went to the bathroom with his comics to do his duty.

Next thing you know, we heard him yelling and screaming that he's bleeding and about to die.

We went into the bathroom and saw his legs and the walls were covered with red stuff that looked like blood.

Creepy got up real up close to it, smelled it, and then licked it.

"Eeewwww," was all we could say.

"Hey guys, its only ketchup," Creepy said.

58

Then we lifted the toilet seat and found about fifty ketchup packets that Nick had put under there.

Man, camp life is hard.

Saturday

Steve finally made it to the Swamp Biome today.

He was all covered in brown and green paint, and had a green bandana around his head.

60

I could tell he was ready for war.

"Steve, man, I'm so glad you're here," I said. "Trying to hold down the fort by myself is hard."

"Good job, soldier," he said. "So what do you know so far?"

"Well, first, I think the camp counselors are going to try to put a spell on me, to turn me into one of their minions," I said. "They've been really nice to me, but I know what they're up to."

"How do you know that they haven't put a spell on you already?" Steve asked.

I just looked at him...confused.

"Well, anyway, I found an Enchanted Book in the Stronghold that's near camp, and I thought you could use it to make a protective spell or something around us."

"Yeah, well, my enchantments aren't very good," Steve said. "But we can always ask Glenda, the Swamp Witch to help us. The full moon comes out in a few days, so she'll be back by then."

"Also, the cafeteria food monster eats like twenty kids a day," I said. "And it picks them clean. I haven't seen any body parts or mob kid remains at all."

"Whoa," was all Steve could say.

"So where are you staying?" I asked Steve.

"I built a small dirt house right outside of your camp," he said. "That way I can stay close."

"Awesome."

Man, having Steve around is going to be great.

I was going to ask him to help me with my Nick problem. But I didn't want to distract him from the mission.

Besides, Nick hasn't poisoned anyone yet, so I've got nothing to worry about.

Sunday

BANG! BANG! BANG!

"Wake up, campers!" was all I heard, as I
tried to get out of bed.

Then I saw Endy next to the camp counselor
crying.

"Somebody is in real trouble," the camp
counselor said. "One of you poisoned this
Enderman's pet Endermites. And no one is
leaving until I find out who it was."

Nick, the Wither Skeleton, gave me mean
look. Then he made a sign with his fingers
into the shape of a book.

I guess he was trying to tell me that if I didn't
take the blame, he was going to tell everyone
about the Enchanted Book.

64

"It was me," I said. "I poisoned the Endermites as a prank."

"Zombie, how could you?" Endy ran out of the cabin crying.

I felt terrible.

"Well, Zombie, you're in a lot of trouble," the counselor said. "We're going to have to call your parents, and you're going to be on cafeteria clean-up duty for the rest of camp."

Cafeteria clean-up? That means I'm going to be the cafeteria monster's next meal!

Nick just looked at me and smiled.

Monday

Yesterday the camp called my parents and they were so disappointed.

"What were you thinking son?" Dad said, and Mom added, "We raised you better than that."

I could hear my little brother giggling in the background.

I felt so bad because I couldn't tell them the truth. But I really needed the Enchanted Book to help save the camp.

Now, I should probably be worried about trying to find a way out from under Nick's thumb.

But I've got bigger things to worry about.

Today is my first day on cafeteria duty.

And I'm really scared.

I wonder what it feels like to be eaten. Probably feels like getting thrown into a trash compactor. Or maybe if feels like falling into a meat grinder. A wood chipper maybe?

I'm so doomed.

When I walked into the cafeteria, the head cook was waiting to greet me.

"Hi there, you must be Zombie," he said. "My name is Flavio, and I am the head chef at Cobblestone Camp."

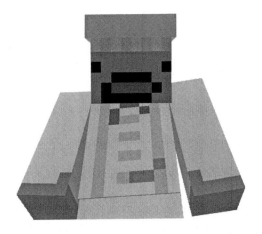

He was a Zombie, but he had an accent, so I think he was from the Mesa Biome.

"Hi, it's good to meet you," I said, not sure if I could trust this guy.

I mean, he's been working this long around the cafeteria food monster and hasn't been eaten.

Either he's a real tough mob, or he's the one holding the legs of the kids as they go down the monster's stomach.

He didn't look that tough to me, so he must be working for the monster.

"I need you to helb me prepare everyone's breakfass, young Zombie," he said. "Here, you hold the pot and I get the meats."

What?

All of a sudden, Flavio goes into the refrigerator and starts unwrapping some meat products.

Those must be the remains from all of the mob kids! I thought. *No wonder I couldn't find any. He's taking the left overs and feeding them back to the kids!*

I started feeling dizzy.

"Hey Zombie, are you OK?"

All of a sudden, I hurled into the big pot.

"Hey! You discovered my secret ingreedient. Thank you, you saved me trouble of adding it myself. You are such a great helb."

I couldn't hold it in, and I hurled again.

"Huepa!" he yelled.

Tuesday

Today I got a little break from activities thanks to my cafeteria experience.

But I had that dream again.

This time, I was tied up and couldn't move. The camp counselors carried me to an altar to sacrifice me to the cafeteria food monster.

Down below, the cafeteria food monster was as big as a mountain with a giant mouth, gurgling down all of the poor mob camp kids.

Before they got me to the altar, poor Endy was thrown in. Then Flapper was thrown in. Then Creepy was thrown in.

The camp counselors are all laughing and relishing the moment.

Then I got to the altar and they were about to throw me in. Before the masked altar person threw me in, he took off his mask…and it was Nick!

He grinned from ear to ear and then pushed me off the altar into the monster's mouth.

As I was falling, all I could think about was how I was never going to see my parents again, or my ghoulfriend Sally, or even my pesky little brother.

Then, all of a sudden I hear, "HHHEEEIIIIIIAAAAAAHHHH!!!"

In a blaze of glory, Steve, with a vine tied around his leg, bungee cord jumped into the cafeteria food monster's mouth, and caught me before I got swallowed whole.

We bounced up to the tree he was tied to, but as I looked down, I saw my buddies among the crowd of mob kids being swallowed.

I tied a vine around my ankle, and Steve and I both jumped in to save our friends.

Steve grabbed and saved Endy, and I saved Flapper.

But, as I looked down to prepare to get Creepy, he shook his head no.

Then Creepy started to hiss, and flash, and then, "KKKKAABBBOOOOOMMM!"

Creepy blew up, and the other creeper campers blew up, and they blew up the entire cafeteria food monster and all of the camp counselors with it.

Then I woke up.

Man, did I just see the future?

I've got to do everything I can to never let that happen, I thought.

I met up with Steve later in the day and I told him about my dream.

"Whoa," Steve said. "Maybe it was the future…"

"That means we need to do something soon, or we're all doomed," I said.

"Yeah, we really need to go see Glenda, the Swamp Witch," Steve said. "But the full moon isn't till next week."

"We'll all be zombie burgers by next week," I said nervously. "Remember, I've got to work at the cafeteria all week, so you know I'm gonna be next."

"Man, if only we had some gunpowder, we could make some TNT blocks," Steve said as he looked at me funny.

"Don't even think about it. Creepy's my friend, you know."

"What?" Steve said smiling.

So I went back to my cabin, hopeless.

Wednesday

Today was Care Package Day.

It's when all of the campers receive care packages from their parents.

Parents aren't always the coolest bunch, but they make up for it in care packages.

I thought my parents were definitely going to forget my care package, since they were so disappointed in me because of the Endermite incident.

But, they came through!

They actually sent me my favorite snacks: cookies, milk, dried zombie boogers and cake!

Endy got some cool blocks. He got some cobblestone blocks, some dirt blocks, some gravel blocks and even some obsidian.

I asked him what they were for and he said that they were for picking up and moving around.

I just looked at him...confused.

Flapper's parents sent him some sponges, prismarine crystals, and a target with a bull's-eye.

I asked Flapper what the target was for, and he showed me. He put it about five feet away from him and then he stared at it for a few seconds.

All of a sudden, BOOM! A laser beam came out of his big eye and knocked the target right over.

"Whoa! I didn't know you could do that."

"Yeah, it's a gift," Flapper said.

Creepy's parents sent him another liquid Nitrogen inhaler and some baby powder. He also got some shirts and pants, which is weird because the shirts had arm holes and the pant legs were really long.

I still don't think Creepy's parents understand him very well. It's probably why he walks around naked all of the time.

I kind of felt bad that Creepy didn't get any cool toys and stuff so I went over to see how he was doing.

"Hey Creepy," I said, "How's it going?"

"Great!" he said. "My Mom and Dad sent me my favorite stuff!"

Wow. Didn't see that coming.

"Really? You like this stuff?"

"Yeah. My favorite is the baby powder. It keeps me from getting itchy in the middle of the night," he said.

"What's it made of?" I asked him.

"Gunpowder," he said. "It's the only kind of powder that Creepers use."

Did he just say what I think he said?

Oh man, this is so on!

Steve is going to be so pumped when he finds out we can make some TNT blocks.

Hey, maybe we can save the day after all...

Thursday

Today I asked Creepy if I could use some of his baby powder.

"Sure," he said. "Just don't use it all. These cabin bunks are real itchy."

So I tried to not take too much so that Creepy wouldn't notice.

I went to go see Steve and showed him what I got.

"Hmmm. That's only enough to make a small TNT block," he said. "We just need to put it where it's going to do the most damage."

"I know!" I said excitedly. "Tomorrow all the campers and counselors are going to be outside all night to look at the stars and tell stories and stuff."

"Awesome, we just need to get the counselors by themselves and BOOM! We're home free," he said.

"But how are we going to get them by themselves?"

"Leave that to me," he said with a creepy look on his green and brown face.

Friday

Today we had a campfire with all of the campers and counselors.

The head camp counselor, Jerry, started telling some scary stories.

He started telling stories about humans that used to live in the woods and would attack unsuspecting mob kids and eat their brains.

He said that it was in this very camp, Camp Cobblestone, that the humans attacked, and it was the first Human Apocalypse that claimed the brains of hundreds of mob campers.

All of the mob kids were terrified. I've got to admit, my knees started knocking just thinking about it.

Then it hit me.

Tonight's the night that they're going to sacrifice us to the cafeteria food monster!

What better time than when they have all of the mob kids in one place.

Then I got up like I was going to the bathroom, and I snuck into the woods to find Steve.

"Steve, it's tonight!" I said, "They're going to sacrifice us to that monster tonight!"

"Well, then we need to make this count," he said.

"How are you going to get all of the counselors by themselves?" I asked him.

"Well, since they're brain eating humans in disguise, I'm going to go out there and tell them I'm on their side," he said. "Then I'm going to trick them into doing a huddle so we can discuss the evening menu, then BOOM!"

I thought about what he said, and I couldn't help thinking...

Steve is such a genius! I definitely want to be stuck with him during a Human Apocalypse.

Right when Steve and I got back to the campers, Jerry was finishing his story.

And, the humans are said to have been buried in these woods. But on nights like tonight, they have been known to crawl out of their graves, to wreak their revenge on the next group of young, delicious, campers that would be brave enough to step foot in Camp Cobblestone!

Right then, Steve jumped out of the woods and yelled, "My name is Steve and I am human! I am here to feast on these delicious campers with you!"

The entire camp went wild.

There was yelling and screaming and mob kids and counselors running all over the place.

They were running up trees, running into the woods, and running into each other.

I saw Zombie body parts flying, as well as skeleton skulls, and Slime bits scattered everywhere.

There were Endermen kids teleporting all over the place, as well as Zombies turning white.

I even saw a few Zombie camp counselors actually jump in the water, and try to swim their way to safety. And if you didn't know, zombies and water don't usually mix.

A lot of mob kids got hurt, but the most important thing was that we saved the kids from being eaten, and we saved the camp.

And we didn't even need to use the TNT.

Today, victory was ours!

Saturday

Today they decided not to have any activities because all of the campers were at the Nurse's office getting stitched up and put back together.

I still wasn't sure about whose side Nurse Golem was on, so I just kept an eye on her.

At our cabin, all the guys stayed in bed most of the day, just moaning and groaning about everything that happened.

"That was the scariest night of my life," Flapper said.

"Yeah, I used up both bottles of my liquid Nitrogen inhaler," Creepy said.

"I was so scared, I couldn't even move," Endy said. "All I could do what stand there and stare."

"How about you, Zombie?" Creepy asked, "Weren't you scared?"

"Uh, yeah, sure," I said, trying to act scared.

"Man, did you see the camp counselors run away like chickens?" Nick asked. "Those guys are real wimps."

That was weird, I thought. *I was sure that the camp counselors would've accepted Steve as one of their own.*

"Yeah…wimps," I said.

Sunday

Today, everything went back to normal.

I think the camp counselors thought they could take our minds off of the crazy events from the other night by keeping us busy.

They're probably setting up to try again, I thought.

Today most of the camp kids were practicing for the talent show or doing crafts.

Creepy was still a bit sick from having inhaled two bottles of liquid Nitrogen, so he stayed in the cabin.

Endy, Flapper and I started practicing for our band. And boy did we sound terrible.

When we got back to our cabin, Creepy was in his bunk sleeping.

"Hey, don't worry about it, guys," Flappy said. "I'm sure with a little practice we'll sound real good."

"But we still need a singer," Endy said.

"You need somebody to play guitar too, because I'm terrible," I said.

Then Nick walked in the cabin.

"Hey guys, did you hear the dying Mooshroom cow wailing earlier?" he said. "Oh, wait, that was you guys!"

Then he started laughing.

"OK, so we're bad," Flappy said. "But I bet Creepy's drums will probably help us sound a whole lot better."

That didn't make me feel any better.

Later, I saw Steve at our usual spot.

"Hey Zombie, what's bugging you?" Steve asked.

"Botflies, I think," I said.

"No, what's bothering you?" Steve said.

"Oh, we're trying to put a band together for our talent show, and we sound terrible," I said. "By the way, do you sing?"

"Nope, but I play a mean electric guitar," he said.

I just smiled back at him.

"But we've got more important things to worry about," he said. "The campfire was our first victory, but I think they're going to try again."

"You're right," I said. "What are we going to do?"

"Only thing we can do is bring your Enchanted Book to Glenda, the Swamp Witch, to see if she can use it to put a protection spell on us and the other mob kids."

"Do you think it'll work?" I asked.

"It has to, it's our only hope," he said.

"Well, at least we have the TNT," I said.

Steve just looked at me with a weird smile and said, "Did you see my new diamond? I just mined it last night."

Oh brother...

Monday

Today they made an announcement that even after the craziness from the other night, we were still going to have the Moblympics.

They said they were going to do the drawing for it tomorrow.

I didn't really know what the Moblympics were, so I asked Creepy about it.

"Well, remember the obstacle course we did when we first got here?" Creepy said. "Just imagine that, but bigger."

"Does everybody have to participate?" I asked Creepy.

"Well, they usually have a drawing to pick a cabin from our camp, to go and battle a cabin from Camp Nether Rack," Creepy said. "But don't worry. I've been coming to camp for three years, and they've never picked Cabin Zero, which is our cabin. Some kids think they only draw from the cabins with the most athletic mob kids."

That was a relief. I didn't want to go through that traumatic experience on the Vine Cross again.

Tuesday

"**A**nd the winning cabin, who will go on to the Moblympics...is Cabin Zero!"

Those were the last words I heard at roll call this morning. Everything else was a blur after that.

I saw Creepy later at our cabin, and I asked him, "I thought you said our cabin never gets picked!"

"It doesn't, I don't know what happened," he said. "Maybe they think you or Endy are athletic."

Then I looked over at Nick in his bunk, and I knew he had something to do with it.

"You had something to do with us getting picked, didn't you, Nick?"

"Yep, it's about time I paid back those Nether Rack Cretans for kicking me out," he said.

"How are we supposed to win this thing?" I asked him. "None of us are athletic."

"I don't care if we win," he said. "I'm just going to make sure they never forget it."

So in a few days, we're going to the Moblympics. Then we're going to be arrested as accessories to Nick's murder spree.

Can things get any worse?

Wednesday

Well, today was Parent's Day.

So I had to face my Mom and Dad's disappointing faces.

Not to mention, they made me apologize to Endy's parents, which was also really embarrassing.

I just have to keep remembering my mission. And when it's all over I'll tell them the truth, and then they will all understand why.

I got to meet Flapper's parents, who were visiting from the Ocean Biome. Flapper's Dad is an Elder Guardian, which means that he's important and stuff. I think he works in the Ocean Monument or something.

And Creepy's parents I knew really well, so it was good seeing them.

But when I looked over at Nick, I saw that he was all alone.

"Hey Creepy," I said, "how come Nick's parents didn't make it?"

"Nick's parents never come to camp," Creepy said. "Every year on Parent's Day he just sits in the hall all by himself."

Man, that must be tough, I thought. *I don't know how I would feel if my Mom and Dad didn't come visit me in this prison camp.*

So I decided to go talk to Nick. Knowing him, though, he's probably going to act tough and stuff. But Billy the counselor gave me an idea about how to make him feel better.

"Waddup?" I said to Nick.

"What do you want, Cretan?"

"Nick, I have a question for you," I said.

"What is it?" He sounded annoyed.

"Why was the Zombie afraid to cross the road?"

"Why?" he said

"Because he lost his guts!"

"PFFFFTTTT! That was the stupidest joke I ever heard," he said laughing.

I started laughing too.

"Oh, yeah? What do you call a Zombie with a lot of kids?" he asked.

"What?"

"A MOMster!"

"Classic!" I said.

"How about this one: What is a Zombie's favorite toy?"

"What?"

"A DEADY bear!"

"Oh, yeah, what kind of games do baby Zombies play?"

"What?"

"CORPSE and Robbers!"

We went on like this for a while. I could tell it was making Nick feel better.

Before I left him to go say goodbye to my folks, he told me, "You know what, Zombie, you're alright."

It was the weirdest thing, but I think Nick and I can actually be friends. That is, if he doesn't poison me in the middle of the night.

Why does that happen to Nick anyway?

I wonder...

Thursday

Today was a full moon, so after camp activities, I met up with Steve to pay a visit to Glenda, the Swamp Witch. I brought the enchantment book with me too, to see if she could help us use it.

When we got there, there was a light in the window of her Witch's Hut, so we knew she was home.

"I hope she doesn't feed us those rotten flesh meatballs she did last time we were here," I said.

"I don't know," Steve said. "I thought they were kind of tasty."

"Wha..?"

"Just kidding," he said.

We knocked on the door to the hut, and we heard her say, "Steve, Zombie, come in. Just close the door behind you, I'm in the kitchen."

"How did she it know it was us?" I said.

"Well, she is a witch, you know."

Glenda is a witch, but she's the weirdest witch I have ever seen. She didn't wear a black hat or have a big nose with a mole on it.

I wonder if I should ask her why she looks so different, I thought. Naah, she'll just turn me into a frog or something for asking.

We walked into her hut and went to the kitchen, and Glenda was busy making cookies.

"Hi Zombie! Hello Steve! You're both looking well," she said.

"Hi, Witch Glenda," Steve and I both said.

"Would you like a cookie?" she asked.

I wasn't sure if I should take one. But by the time I finished thinking about it, Steve ate about three of them.

"What can I do for you boys?" she asked.

"Well, we need to know how to use this Enchanted Book so that we can put a protective spell on ourselves and the other campers, so that we can battle the Zombie eating witch, the rotten flesh eating camp counselors, and the cafeteria food monster," I said, out of breath.

"Wow, that is a mouthful," she said.

"Yeh, we wanf to desfroy the momsturs beefur they get us," Steve said with a mouth full of cookies.

"What was that?" Glenda asked.

"He said, we want to destroy the monsters before they get us," I said.

Glenda just looked at us with a look that said, *you boys are so cute and so dumb at the same time.* Kind of like when you look at a puppy.

Then she asked, "How do you know they are monsters?"

"Because..." Then I just stopped for a moment. How *did* we know?

"Well, what made you *think* they were monsters?" she asked.

"Well, I had this dream and, it seemed so real, and they took away my computer and video games, and..." I said.

Me and Steve just looked at each other... confused. Then we scratched our heads and together said, "Oooohhh."

"So when the camp counselors were being nice to me, they were really being nice?" I said.

"Hmm Hmm," she said.

"And the reason I didn't see any mob kid body parts, in the cafeteria was because there weren't any?" I said.

"Hmm Hmm," she said.

"And the reason Nurse Golem and Billy the counselor were so nice was because they really liked me?" I said, feeling really dumb.

Steve was still eating cookies, when all of a sudden...

"PFFFFTTTTT!" he spit out all of the cookies and fell to the floor laughing.

I just stood there, feeling really dumb.

"Don't worry, Zombie, we have all mistaken other people for monsters, and we've even been mistaken for monsters ourselves."

Right when she said that I thought about Nick. After spending time with him yesterday, I realized he wasn't such a monster after all.

Speaking of Nick, I wonder...

"Witch Glenda," I asked. "Can you use this Enchanted Book to help a Wither Skeleton that can't control his poison?"

"You know, Zombie," she said. "That problem is more common than you think among Wither Skeleton boys. It usually happens during puberty when a Wither Skeleton boy is under a lot of stress."

"Really," I said.

"The best remedy is to help him have some fun," she said. "And you don't need an Enchanted Book for that."

"Whoa," Steve and I both said.

"Thanks, Witch Glenda," I said. "And here," I added as I gave her the Enchanted book. "I don't think I'll be needing this anymore."

Steve and I said goodbye to Glenda. Steve tried to raise his hand but his arms were full of cookies.

"Wow, Steve," I said. "I was so wrong about camp. I guess it's not so bad here after all."

"Yeah, a lot of kids say that," he said. "They usually hate it until they get there and find out it's a lot of fun. Crazy, right?"

"Yup," I said as we walked back to the camp site, eating some delicious cookies on the way.

Friday Morning Entry

Today is the first day of the Moblympics, and I'm adding this journal entry because I don't know if I'm going to make it back alive.

Creepy on the other hand is really excited that he finally got picked to go.

Endy hasn't talked to me since he thought I poisoned his Endermites. Really hurts, though, because I really liked him.

Flapper is busy doing his jumping jacks to get ready for the events. I never saw a Guardian do jumping jacks before, so I tried not to laugh.

I walked over to Nick to see what he was doing. He had a big black bag full of swords, axes, pickaxes, TNT and other weapons.

"Hey Nick, can I talk to you for a second?" I said.

"What is it, Zombie?"

"Hey, I know you're going to go destroy the Camp Nether Rack kids, and burn their whole camp to the ground and stuff…" I said.

"What's your point?" he said.

"Hey, would you mind doing it at the end of the Moblympics? The guys are really excited about being picked to go to this. And Creepy's been coming to camp for three years, and thanks to you, it's the first time he's been picked for anything."

Nick looked at Endy and Creepy, then he looked at Flapper, and tried not to laugh.

"Yeah, sure," he said. "It doesn't matter when those Camp Nether Rack Cretans get what's coming to them, just that they do. But you don't think we can win this thing, do you?"

"Well, if we win, we can humiliate them, and you can blow them up after," I said.

Then Nick made a really big smile.

Friday Night Entry

Well, today was the craziest day ever!

All I can say is that I am so proud to be part of the gang in Cabin Zero.

When we got to the Moblympics, the place was a real mob. All the mob kids from both camps were there and it was really loud.

As for the course, that place looked like a scene from Zombie Ninja Warrior.

Kinda don't think they understand we're only kids.

Well, the kids from Camp Nether Rack were real tough. They kinda looked hand-picked to me.

There was a Ghast, a Blaze, a Zombie Pigman, a Magma Cube and lastly, there was a Wither Skeleton who was really huge.

For the Moblympics, there were five events altogether. Three events today, and two events tomorrow.

The five events were the Telephone Pole, the Potato sack race, the Vine Cross, the Rope Climb, and the Mud Run.

They did a random drawing for each event, and of course, I got the Vine Cross.

Endy got the Telephone Pole, Creepy got the rope climb (which I was really worried about), Flapper got the Potato Sack race (which worried me too), and Nick got the Mud Run.

Only rule for the games was that we couldn't use our abilities. That worked good for us, since Endy didn't know how to teleport yet.

First, Endy and the Ghast had to climb the Telephone Pole. I thought Endy would win this one easy, but Endy didn't know how to

114

climb that well either. I guess his long arms and legs get in the way.

So Endy struggled to get up the pole. Meanwhile, the Ghast easily used his tentacles to grab one peg at a time.

But all of a sudden, Endy started getting the hang of it and he started to catch up to the Ghast! Next thing we know, they're neck and neck, even though the Ghast didn't have a neck.

And when it was all over, Endy won by a finger! (I know, I didn't even knew Endermen had fingers.)

What was really crazy, was that the Ghast got real mad and knocked Endy off of his telephone pole. We were all standing there with our mouths open as he fell down. But right before he hit the ground, we hear, *"BAMF!"*

Endy teleported!

He teleported to the ground safely. And everybody cheered him on.

BAMF! BAMF! BAMF! BAMF! He was just so happy he could teleport, he did it like ten times before he got tired.

Then it was Flapper's turn. I was still worried about Flapper doing the Potato Race, since he didn't have any arms or legs. But I didn't feel so bad when I saw he was up against the Blaze, who didn't have arms or legs either.

"On your mark, get set, go!"

Flapper quickly jumped inside of his Potato sack, and started flapping up and down toward the finish line. Man, I could not believe that he could see through that thing, but it was like he had X-ray vision or something. He hopped and hopped, getting closer and closer to the finish line.

116

The Blaze just stood there with his potato sack at his feet. Flapper was about half way to the finish line when all of a sudden, the Blaze started spinning around. He created enough hot air that the bag inflated. There was a metal wire attached to him and the potato sack so the potato sack wouldn't fly away. Next thing we know, the Blaze is just walking his potato sack to the finish line like a balloon.

Before Flapper could get to the finish line, the Blaze had beaten him really quick.

Somebody complained that the Blaze cheated, but the judges said that a level of creativity was allowed. So the metal wire and the air poofing of the potato sack was allowed.

Next it was my turn.

I was so scared of the Vine Cross that my
knees were knocking again.

Tock, Tock, Tock.

My knees sounded like a grandfather clock.

Creepy came over and reminded me,
"Remember, Zombie, just think of something
funny and all your fears will go away."

I looked in the crowd and I saw Billy, the
camp counselor, giving me a thumbs up.

I just started thinking of Billy's headless body
being stuck on that vine for two days, and I
started laughing.

I felt much better.

It was me against the Zombie Pigman. He
reminded me a little of my cousin Piggy, but
he was bigger.

Both of our vines were next to each other. And when I looked over, the Zombie Pigman guy gave me a really mean look.

"Go!" was all I heard as I saw the Zombie Pigman start climbing across the vine like he was on fire or something.

I decided to take my time and pace myself.

"One, two, one, two, one, two," was all I said to myself.

I'm doing it! I thought, as I started moving really fast.

I thought the Zombie Pigman dude was definitely going to win since he was going so fast. But then all of a sudden I looked over and I saw his feet, and then his body and then I saw his head next to me.

He was frozen with fear.

This is my chance to beat him! I thought.

So I started moving faster and faster and then I passed him. *I'm going to win!* I thought.

But, as I was moving, I thought, *man, this isn't right.*

So I climbed back to where he was.

"Hey Pig-dude, why was the Zombie afraid to cross the road?"

"Wwwhhyy?"

"Because he didn't have any guts!"

The Zombie Pig-dude let out a small laugh, and I could tell he felt better.

"What do you say we finish this race?" I told him.

"Sounds good," he said.

So we both climbed the vine together to finish the race. Zombie Pig-dude was totally better than me at the Vine cross, so he won the race.

But, even though I lost, I still felt great.

Today was awesome!

I'm just so proud of the guys in my cabin.

And who knows, tomorrow, we may even win this thing.

Saturday

Creepy has arms!!!

I can't believe it!

All this time, I've felt really sad for Creepy because he didn't have any arms. And today I found out that not only does he have arms, but he has legs too!

When Creepy's rope climbing event was about to start, I wanted to prepare him so he wouldn't be disappointed.

"Creepy, don't worry about this event, man. If you don't win, it was just great that we got picked for the Moblympics."

"Uh-huh."

"I mean, you know, not everybody is built for these things. Look at Flapper. Poor guy has got to flap around all over the..."

"Go!"

In the middle of my sentence, Creepy's event started. Creepy ran up to the rope and took a quick look at the top. Then he stared at the rope like he was becoming one with it.

Then out of nowhere, Creepy's back leg stumps got sucked into his body, and then out popped these two beefy arms out of Creepy's sides. Then his last two leg stumps started growing into two long legs.

Creepy has arms and legs! I dropped my jaw, literally.

Then Creepy started climbing the rope like he was born in the Jungle Biome. He made it to the top in three minutes flat.

The Wither Skeleton was so shocked by what he saw, that by the time he got on the rope, Creepy had already won the race.

Creepy strutted over to me, really proud.

"How come you never told me you had arms and legs?" I asked.

"You never asked," he said with a big smile on his face.

"Whoa," was all I could say.

So, everything was tied.

It was up to Nick to win this thing for us.

I went over to see Nick before his event started.

"Hey Nick," I said.

"What's up, Zombie," he said as he stretched his Wither Skeleton legs.

"Hey, I know you don't have to really try, since you're probably going to burn everything down to the ground later, but it would really mean a lot to me and the guys if you could smoke this guy," I said.

"Hey, Zombie," Nick said. "There's something I've wanted to tell you for a couple of days now, and it's about time I tell you."

125

"What is it?" I asked nervously.

"I can sing, you know," he said, and then the gun went off for his event.

Nick moved like a stone in the mud because it was so thick.

The Magma Cube had a really strong jump, so for every few feet Nick moved, the Magma Cube caught up and passed him.

But then all of a sudden something happened to Nick. I could tell he was crying. Then, out of nowhere, he took off like he was walking on water. He started running like he had waited all of his life to run like this.

The Magma Cube couldn't jump that far and finally got really tired and fell down into the mud.

Nick won the race, and we won the Moblympics!

126

We all went over to Nick to congratulate him.

Except this time, it wasn't the tough and hard Nick that we were congratulating. Something happened to him during the Mud Run. He was smiling from ear to ear.

All of the guys, including Creepy this time, lifted Nick up in the air, and we carried him away celebrating.

After the games, we all went to the Camp Cobblestone cafeteria where Flavio presented us with the biggest cake I have ever seen.

On the cake it said:

CONGRACHULACHUNS, CAMP SERO!

Man, I never thought I would say this, but camp is the best thing ever!

127

Sunday

Well, yesterday was the first time Cabin Zero ever won the Moblympics in the past 22 years.

And it felt awesome.

What was really awesome was all the cake we ate after the games.

Flavio's cake was *soooooo* good.

Also, Nick is a completely different kid now. He told Endy and the camp counselors the truth about poisoning the Endermites.

The camp counselors called my parents and told them what really happened, which was a relief. Endy also forgave me, which really made me happy too.

The good thing is that Nick is so happy now, I don't think he'll be poisoning anybody else for a long time.

...that is until he gets to high school.

Tonight, we're going to have our talent show, and our band is finally complete. Nick is going to be our lead singer, Endy is going to play the Note Blocks, Creepy is going to play drums, Flapper is playing the tambourines, and I'm playing guitar.

Yeah, I know. I can't play the guitar. But I don't think anyone is going to care, because I have Steve behind the curtains playing a real electric guitar.

I'm just going to carry my guitar, and dazzle them with my amazing air guitar skills.

Bring it!

Monday

Well, today we're going home.

I'm really sad, though. Because these last three weeks have been the best three weeks of my entire life.

I'm really going to miss the new best friends I made.

Endy was really happy to tell his parent's he can teleport now. I think he also said that he's going to visit the Enderworld to learn more about his family history.

Flappy went back to the Ocean Biome. He said that he got tired of the dry air and wanted something more humid.

I found out that Nick lives really close to where my cousin Piggy lives, in the Nether.

So hopefully I'll see him when my family goes out to visit my cousin's family.

And Creepy is coming home with me back to our town. Except now, I think he's going to show more people his *other* side.

As for me, I learned so much at camp that I can't wait to go home and ask my Mom and Dad to sign me up for camp next year.

So now, I have a few more weeks until school starts, which means that I can finally have my 24/7 video game and cake marathon I've been waiting so long for.

…that is, unless my parents planned some unexpected, unwanted trip that I really don't want to go on.

Naah, they would never do that…

Find out What Happens Next in...

Diary of a Minecraft Zombie Book 7
"Zombie Family Reunion"

Get Your Copy and Join Zombie on More Exciting Adventures!

Leave Us a Review

Please support us by leaving a review. The more reviews we get the more books we will write!

And if you really liked this book, please tell a friend. I'm sure they will be happy you told them about it.

Check Out Our Other Books from Zack Zombie Publishing

The Diary of a Minecraft Zombie
Book Series

Get The Entire Series on
Amazon Today!

135

The Ultimate Minecraft Comic Book Series

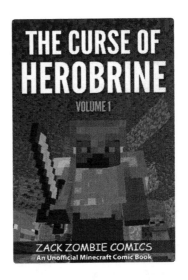

Get The Entire Series on Amazon Today!

Herobrine's Wacky Adventures

Get The Entire Series on Amazon Today!

The Mobbit
An Unexpected Minecraft Journey

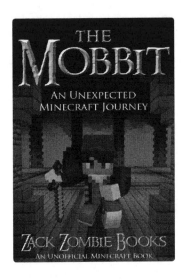

Get The Entire Series on
Amazon Today!

Steve Potter and the
Endermen's Stone

Get The Entire Series on
Amazon Today!

An Interview With a
Minecraft Mob

Get The Entire Series on
Amazon Today!

Minecraft
Galaxy Wars

Get The Entire Series on
Amazon Today!

Ultimate Minecraft Secrets:

An Unofficial Guide to Minecraft Tips, Tricks and Hints to Help You Master Minecraft

Get Your Copy on Amazon Today!